The Pilgrim's Progress

D0308788

A Gift from

East Sheen

Baptist Church

Telephone: 0208 876 2321

www.eastsheenbaptist.org

The Pilgrim's Progress

JOHN BUNYAN'S
ORIGINAL STORY
RETOLD BY

Jean Watson

CF4·K

10 9 8 7 6 5 4 3 2

The Pilgrim's Progress ISBN 978-1-84550-459-5
© Copyright 2009 Jean Watson
Reprinted 2013

Published in 2009 by Christian Focus Publications, Geanies House,
Fearn, Tain, Ross-shire, IV20 1TW,
Scotland, U.K.
Fact files: © Copyright Christian Focus Publications

Cover design: Daniel van Straaten
Cover illustration: Vic Mitchell
Interior illustrations: Vic Mitchell,
Tim Charnick

Think about it; Bible Search;
Find out the Facts © Copyright Christian Focus Publications
Printed and bound in Denmark
by Nørhaven

Contents

The Book.................................. 7

The Gate 19

The Cross.............................. 33

The Fight.............................. 43

The Battle with Apollyon 51

The Valley of Shadow.................... 59

Vanity Fair............................. 73

A New Friend 87

Doubting Castle 97

The Mountains 107

A Testing Time......................... 119

The City 129

Find out the Facts 140

New Words and Ideas................... 143

The Book

Once upon a time, there was a man called Christian who lived in the City of Destruction with his wife and four children. He wasn't very rich but he worked quite hard and earned enough money to buy all the food and clothes which his family needed. He had a smart little wooden house and plenty of friends and neighbours to gossip with, and for a long time he was really happy. Then one day he found the book.

It was lying on the floor of his attic – covered in dust and cobwebs. He picked it up and rubbed the dirt off the cover with his sleeve.

It looked very old. He sat down on a box and started to read it.

Poor Christian! The book he'd found was very frightening. Before he had read two pages, he was shaking all over, and by the time he'd reached the end, he was in tears.

'My wife and children mustn't see me like this,' he thought. 'I'd better go outside and give myself time to calm down.' He closed the book and tried to stand up – but he couldn't. There seemed to be a heavy weight pulling at his shoulders and dragging him back.

'What's the matter?' he wondered in alarm. He put his hands behind him and started feeling around. Soon his groping fingers made out the shape of a huge, knobbly sack on his back. It was strapped to his waist and shoulders but, however hard he tried, he could not get it off.

'This is terrible! What am I going to do?' he thought. He tried to stand up again, and this time he just managed it. Then, puffing and panting, he got himself out of the house without being seen.

He paced up and down the garden, hoping the fresh air would make him feel better. But it didn't. The trouble was, he couldn't forget his burden, or his book – which he kept stopping to re-read, even though it upset him so much. When he went back indoors, he was in tears again.

Christian's wife saw him hurrying past the kitchen and called out, 'Why, whatever's the matter with you? And what's that thing on your back?'

'Oh, nothing, nothing!' Christian answered, trying to sound cheerful. But it was no use. Before long, his real feelings showed, and he had to explain why he was in such a state.

'I have just had some very bad news,' he said, looking sadly at his wife and children. 'One day, perhaps very soon, a terrible fire is going to sweep right through our city and burn everything up.'

The children hardly had time to feel frightened before their mother laughed and said, 'Whatever gave you that crazy idea?'

'I read it in this book,' Christian replied, holding it up.

'You can't believe all that you read!' exclaimed his wife.

'But it's true,' insisted Christian. 'Ever since I read about it, I've had this heavy pack on my back and felt miserable and worried.'

'You're just over-tired,' said his wife, firmly. 'And as soon as I've put the children to bed, I'm going to make sure that you get a nice early night.'

The children decided there was no need to be frightened, as their mother wasn't, so they went to bed happily. Not long afterwards, Christian's wife bundled her husband into bed, telling him that he would feel quite different after a good sleep. But she was wrong.

Christian didn't sleep a wink, and in the morning he was as miserable as ever. His wife looked at his long face and began to feel just a little annoyed with him.

'You really must try to pull yourself together,' she told him. 'You'll frighten the children! And what will the neighbours think?'

'Please read this book,' Christian begged her, but she replied crossly, 'Certainly not! If you want to be miserable – go ahead, but don't expect *me* to join you!'

After that she kept well out of his way, and made sure that the children didn't come near him either.

Christian now felt very lonely, as well as sad. He spent the next few days all by himself, either in his room or walking up and down some nearby fields. Sometimes, he prayed to God for help, and sometimes he studied the book which he now took everywhere with him. And all the time there was a lump of misery inside him and a lump of guilt on his back.

During one of his walks, he met a man known as Evangelist. This gentleman came straight up to Christian and asked, 'Why are you so upset?'

'Because this book tells me that if I stay here, I will die,' Christian replied.

'Why not leave then?'

'Because I don't know a safe place to go,' Christian said.

'Now that's where I can help you,' Evangelist answered. Christian could hardly believe his ears! Here, at last, was someone who understood how he felt and could tell him what to do.

Evangelist pointed far across the fields and asked, 'Do you see that light?' Christian screwed up his eyes and thought he saw a faint glimmer.

'Yes, I think so,' he said.

'Well, keep walking straight towards it along this path, and before long you will see a gate. Go right up to it and knock, and someone will tell you what to do next.'

'Thank you, thank you!' exclaimed Christian. Then, in spite of the load he was carrying, he started to run — towards the light and away from his home, family and friends.

His wife was looking out of the window and saw what was happening. She rushed out of the front door, shouting, 'Christian, where are you going? Come back! Come back!' But her husband called out, 'I'm going to find life and safety,' and went on running. He knew it would be pointless to go home and try to persuade her to come along too, but he hoped that one day she and the children would follow him.

Hearing all the noise, the neighbours came out of their houses. They, too, called Christian to come back, but he took no notice.

'We've got to stop him – come on!' shouted Obstinate, and he started to chase after Christian.

'Wait for me!' called Pliable, beginning to run, too. His name suited him, because he could be persuaded to try anything new – but it took very little to make him give up. His companion, Obstinate, was just the opposite. He stuck to his opinions, no matter how many people told him he was in the wrong.

These two men quickly caught up with Christian, who was slowed down by the weight on his back.

'We've come to make you see sense and go home,' Obstinate panted.

Christian shook his head.

'You've got a house, a wife, children and lots of friends – what more could you possibly want?' Obstinate demanded.

'I want to live, not die!' Christian answered. 'Come with me to a safe and happy place!'

'I can see it's no use arguing with you in this mood,' said Obstinate, sounding very annoyed. 'Come along, Pliable.'

'But supposing Christian's right?' Pliable asked, hesitating.

'Of course he's not right!' Obstinate answered.

'If you don't believe me, read what my book says,' Christian said earnestly. He looked and sounded so sincere that Pliable was persuaded.

'That settles it. I'll go with Christian,' he said.

'You're a couple of fools!' exclaimed Obstinate. 'Goodbye and good riddance!' With these words, he turned and set off in the direction of his home, while Christian and his new companion walked towards the light.

Christian

Christian, the pilgrim in John Bunyan's story, found an old book one day. What he read in it changed his whole life. He was convinced that the city where he had been living would be destroyed, but he didn't know where to go for safety. Then he met Evangelist and set out on an exciting and dangerous journey towards the heavenly city. Very soon he met people who tried to mislead him.

Perhaps John Bunyan got his idea from a Bible verse like Hebrews chapter 13 verse 14 when he wrote about Christian as a pilgrim in this world. In this Bible verse it tells us that those who believe in Jesus will not be in this world for ever - they are looking for a city which is to come.

Evangelist

Evangelist's job was to guide people to the cross and then on to the heavenly city. He came along at just the right moment, when Christian was in despair and didn't know what to do, and started him off in the right direction. Evangelist wasn't afraid to speak the truth and he could be stern, as well as kind. Christian found *that* out when he stepped off the path later on!

Perhaps John Bunyan chose the name of this character while reading Paul's advice to Timothy in the Bible. You will find it in 2 Timothy chapter 4 verses 1–5.

Think about it:

Are you usually obstinate or pliable? When is it good to stick by your own opinions and when is it wrong? If you are a pliable person what difficulties might you get into?

Do you ever feel burdened like Christian did? Do the wrong things you say and think and do bother you?

Bible Search:

Look up the following Bible verses to find out what you should do about sin:

Psalm 32:5   Psalm 119:11
Romans 6:12   Matthew 26:41
Mark 1:15   Luke 13:5

The Gate

Pliable was, as usual, very excited to be doing something new.

'Tell me about the wonderful things we'll find at the end of our journey,' he urged Christian.

'Gladly,' was the reply. 'It says in my book that we will find an amazing country, ruled over by the greatest of all Princes. God and his angels live there, with all who travelled along this road and arrived ahead of us. When we reach the gates of that place, the Prince will welcome us and we will join the others and be safe and happy for ever and ever.'

'I can't wait! Hurry up, Christian!' exclaimed Pliable.

'I can't go any faster, I'm afraid,' Christian answered, 'because of this pack on my back'

And then it happened. There was a sudden shout from Pliable, who hadn't been looking where he was going, and now found himself knee-deep in mud. Before he could stop himself, Christian had followed him.

The two men had stepped right into a patch of boggy ground lying across their path, and now began to wallow about, sinking lower and lower all the time. Because of the extra weight he was carrying, Christian was even more bogged down than Pliable.

For a few moments, neither of them said anything as they struggled to reach the path. Then Pliable turned round and started going back, shouting, 'If this is the kind of thing we can expect – you can carry on without me!'

As soon as his feet were on firm ground again, Pliable made a beeline for home, leaving Christian still floundering but determined to reach the other side, because he could now see the gate in the distance.

But no matter how hard he tried, Christian could not get himself out of the mud. Instead he became weaker, dirtier, and more desperate each moment. Then he heard a voice.

'Take my hand,' it said. Christian looked up and saw a man with a kind face and an outstretched hand. He reached out his own hand and the stranger's closed round it.

At once, he felt himself being pulled out of the slime and on to firm ground.

'Thank you, thank you, friend!' he gasped.

'My name is Help,' said the man, smiling.

'And mine is Christian,' was the reply. 'I was on my way to that gate when I fell into the swamp – and I was beginning to think that I'd never get out again!'

'Everyone who steps into the Slough of Despond feels like that,' said Help. 'Perhaps that's why very few notice the steps across it.'

'*I* certainly didn't!' said Christian ruefully.

'Well, you're safe now, so you had better be on your way. Goodbye, Christian.'

'Goodbye, Help, and thank you again,' said Christian, as he set off along the path leading to the gate, taking care to watch where he was going.

All went well until a man who had been crossing the fields to the left came up close enough to start a conversation.

'Hullo, my name is Worldly Wiseman,' he said.

'And mine's Christian.'

'You look worn out, my dear fellow. Are you going far?'

'As far as that gate, to begin with,' said Christian.

'Well, if you don't mind my saying so, you'd get along much better without that bulky pack on your back,' remarked Worldly Wiseman.

'Obviously!' said Christian. 'But the point is, I can't get rid of it. That's why I'm going to the gate. A man called Evangelist told me someone there would help me, and he kindly showed me the way, too.'

'He showed you *one* way, and a very dangerous one, as you seem to have discovered already,' replied Worldly Wiseman, looking at the mud still clinging to Christian's legs and clothes. Then he asked, 'Tell me, how did you get that thing on your back in the first place'

'I was reading this book, and suddenly, there it was!'

'Hmm! Just as I thought! That sort of thing is always happening when ordinary people start trying to understand that book!' said Worldly Wiseman knowingly. 'But don't worry. There is an easy way out of your difficulty.'

Christian had an uneasy feeling but he still went on listening to Worldly Wiseman, who pointed to a village just past a nearby hill and said, 'That place is known as Morality. In the very first house lives someone I know, called Legality. Go and see him. He'll have that pack off your back in no time at all.'

Christian was glad to hear that, but he saw that he would have to leave the path in order to reach the village, so he still couldn't make up his mind about what to do.

'Go on!' urged Worldly Wiseman. 'You've got nothing to lose – except your burden! Afterwards, if you don't want to go back to your old home, you could buy a house in the village, send for your wife and children, and settle down there. Prices in Morality are reasonable, and the people decent and friendly – so you couldn't expect to find a better place for making a fresh start in!'

'Sounds fine to me,' said Christian – his mind made up. 'Thank you, and goodbye.'

Then Worldly Wiseman went on his way and Christian stepped off his path and headed for the hill, spurred on by the thought of being free from his burden.

But this hopeful mood did not last long. The nearer he came to the hill, the more afraid he grew and the heavier his load felt.

When he came close enough to observe the huge over hanging ridge under which he would have to pass, he panicked, and stood rooted to the spot – not knowing what to do. It was then that he noticed the flames spurting out of the hillside above him. This confirmed his doubts. He should never have listened to Worldly Wiseman and stepped off the path!

Christian was so frightened when he realised his mistake, that he started sweating and shivering. The last person he wanted to see just then was Evangelist, but this man was now striding towards him. As he came nearer, Christian could see the stern expression on his face and knew exactly what to expect!

Sure enough, Evangelist stopped to lecture Christian about the danger of straying from God's way. His words made the pilgrim feel dreadfully sorry and ashamed. Evangelist noticed this and his face and tone of voice grew gentler.

'You see, Christian,' he explained, kindly, 'the way Worldly Wiseman pointed out to you leads to certain death, sooner or later. And his friend, Legality, has never once managed to remove anyone's burden. There's only one place where people can be set free – and that's at the cross. Worldly Wiseman knows this, but he doesn't like the idea at all. That's why he tried to lure you off the one road which leads straight to the cross.'

'I've made a mess of everything! What can I do?' asked Christian, miserably.

'Because you're sorry for the wrong you have done, you are already forgiven,' Evangelist promised. 'So cheer up, go straight back to the right path – and then stay on it!'

'I will, I promise,' answered Christian.

Evangelist smiled, gave him a quick, warm hug and said, 'Goodbye and God bless you.'

'Goodbye and thank you,' replied Christian, as he turned and hurried back to the path. When he reached it, he began striding along – looking straight ahead and not stopping to speak to anyone on the way. And so he arrived, safely, at the gate. Above it was written 'Knock and the door will be opened to you'. He knocked but there was no answer, so he knocked again and again, calling out, 'Please let me in!'

At last he heard footsteps. Then a voice called out, 'Who are you?' Christian explained who he was and where he was going and the gate began to swing open.

The next moment, he was taken by the hand and pulled quickly inside. The gate clanged shut behind him – not a moment too soon, for almost immediately there was a whistling sound followed by a thud.

Startled, Christian turned to face the man who had let him in.

'I'm Goodwill, the gatekeeper,' the stranger explained. 'And if I hadn't acted quickly, you might have had an arrow in your back. You see, not far from here is an enemy castle owned by Captain Beelzebub. He and his men keep a look-out for people coming to this gate and shoot to kill anyone who tries to get past it.'

Christian thanked Goodwill for rescuing him and answered the questions which the gatekeeper then asked him. Goodwill was very interested to hear the story of Christian's journey so far, and he pointed out the route which the pilgrim must now take.

'Do you see that straight, narrow path?' he asked, looking ahead.

'Yes,' Christian replied. 'Is it straight all the way or are there any bends and side-roads further on? I don't want to get lost.'

'You won't – not if you keep to that path,' answered Goodwill. 'There *are* side-roads, but they are wide and crooked, so you couldn't possibly mistake them for the right way.'

'Good!' said Christian. 'Where does the path lead to?'

'To a very big, beautiful house owned by a man called Interpreter. He'll make you welcome. So spend a few days there and you'll learn a lot.'

'Thank you, I will,' answered Christian. 'Goodbye.'

He left the gatekeeper and hurried along the narrow path until he reached the house. It was, as Goodwill had said, large and beautiful. Feeling a little nervous, he began walking up the long drive.

Pliable

Pliable kept changing his mind. First he thought Obstinate was right, but when he heard what Christian had to say, he decided to travel along with him. Then, after a brief struggle in the Slough of Despond, he changed his mind again!

The people described as rocky ground in the Bible story in Matthew chapter 13 verses 20 and 21 could well have given John Bunyan the idea for the character of Pliable. Can you understand how?

Help

Help came along when Christian was sinking deeper and deeper into the Slough of Despond. He pulled the pilgrim out and set him on his way again. Christian was very grateful to this warm, friendly person, who was willing to stretch out a helping hand when it was needed.

The writer of this story was thinking of Psalm 40 verse 2 in the Bible when he created the character of Help. Can you see why?

Worldly Wiseman

Worldly Wiseman seemed to be just the person Christian needed to meet. He sounded so wise and appeared to know all about burdens and how to get rid of them quickly, and he seemed to know all the right people. Such a man couldn't be wrong, surely! But when Christian stepped off the right path, he wasn't quite so certain about his new friend.

The apostle John writes about people like Worldly Wiseman in the Bible in 1 John chapter 4 verse 5.

Think about it

If someone knocks on a door does that mean that they don't want to see you? Of course it doesn't. When the Bible tells you that Jesus is knocking on the door of your heart, what does that mean? It means that Jesus wants to spend time with you. Jesus longs for his people to be with him. Those who trust in Jesus should long to spend time with him.

Bible Search

The best way to spend time with God is to pray. Look up the following verses to find out what the Bible says about prayer:

Psalm 66:19

Romans 12:12

1 Thessalonians 5:17

1 Peter 4:7

Luke 6:12

Philippians 4:6

1 Peter 3:12

The Cross

Christian reached the front door and knocked. When it was opened, he asked to see the owner and in a few moments Interpreter came. Christian explained who he was and where he was going, and Interpreter welcomed him in and invited him to stay.

The next few days were busy, happy ones for the traveller. The rooms in Interpreter's house were full of surprising people, places and objects and Christian spent some time in several of them, learning things which would help him as he travelled along the road.

One of the first rooms he was shown had nothing in it except a picture hanging on one of its walls. It was the picture of a man with a book in his hands, the world behind his back and a crown above his head. What made the painting so unusual was that the character of the man seemed to shine out of the canvas. His face glowed with love and wisdom, truth and goodness. This was the most wonderful person Christian had ever seen and he couldn't stop looking at him.

'Who is he?' he asked, after a moment or two.

'Your invisible guide,' answered Interpreter, with a smile. 'As you walk along the path, he'll be beside you.'

In another room, Christian saw a parable acted out. Two boys were there – one called Passion and the other Patience. Passion looked sulky and bad-tempered. He was surrounded by toys of all shapes and sizes, which he was playing with very roughly – snatching up first one, then another, and flinging things here and there.

Meanwhile Patience was sitting quietly in his chair. He had no playthings at all. Whenever Passion looked up and saw the boy, he would smile in a gloating, sneering way at him. But Patience didn't seem to notice. He simply went on sitting there, looking as though he were expecting something good to happen and prepared to wait patiently until it did.

'You poor thing!' Passion mocked Patience. 'Look at what you're missing – by just sitting there and waiting!' But his companion made no reply.

Quite suddenly, the scene changed, and now Passion had nothing to gloat about, because all his toys were broken and useless, and he was sitting in the middle of the scattered pieces, looking very glum. His companion was still calm and peaceful.

Interpreter drew Christian to one side to explain the meaning of this parable.

'Passion is like someone wanting his own way and determined to have a good time now. Patience is like someone on his way to heaven. He would rather wait for real joy and treasure than waste time and effort on things that don't last and won't make him really happy.'

Christian saw the point at once and never forgot Passion and Patience. Nor did he ever forget the brave soldier whom he watched, a little later on.

Interpreter took him to a beautiful palace. People in golden robes were walking along its balconies. Christian would have given anything to be one of them! And he wasn't the only one, because the courtyard was full of people – all hoping to get into the palace. The gatekeeper was sitting at a table, with a pen in his hand, writing down their names. But having got past *him*, the people were standing around – too frightened to go any closer to the palace, because of the armed men who were guarding the door.

And then the soldier came into the courtyard. He looked braver and more determined than the others. Striding up to the man at the table he said clearly, 'Write my name down.' The gatekeeper did so and immediately the soldier clapped his helmet on to his head, drew his sword, and charged straight at the armed men.

There followed a fight. The soldier was wounded, but he fought on in spite of this, and at last managed to reach the palace door.

It was opened and he was helped inside. There his wounds were dressed and he was given a golden robe and a warm welcome by the people who lived in the beautiful palace. As Christian stood there, watching all this, he longed to be like the brave man who hadn't let anything stand in his way.

In another room, Christian was shown Backslider in his cage. He was a man who had stepped off the right road to wander where he pleased. But his wanderings had ended in despair and this despair had become an iron cage around him – keeping him inside a prison from which he couldn't escape.

Backslider's misery made Christian sad. So did the sight of Unready in his bedroom, terrified by dreams of Judgement Day.

At last it was time for the pilgrim to be on his way. He said goodbye to Interpreter and set off eagerly – his mind full of all he had heard and seen.

Before long, his path ran between two thick walls. Along these in huge letters was written a word: SALVATION. As he read it, Christian was filled with excitement, for he felt sure he was now close to the place of which Evangelist had spoken: the only place where burdened people could hope for freedom.

At this point, the track which had been smooth and straight became rough and steep, but Christian was so eager to reach the top of the slope that he actually started to run. And then he saw the simple wooden cross.

It stood on the crown of the hill and an open grave lay at the foot. The moment Christian reached the cross, the burden simply fell off his back and on to the ground. Then it rolled down the slope and disappeared from sight into the open grave.

Free at last! He squared his shoulders and stood up straight for the first time. For a moment, he stayed quietly where he was, thinking about the One who had died on the cross so that his burden could be taken away for ever. Tears of joy and gratitude rolled down his face.

Then he noticed three figures coming towards him. They were bright shining beings – angels! They came right up to him and said, 'Peace be with you.'

Then one angel said, 'Your sins are forgiven,' while another gently took away his muddy, tattered clothes and helped him put on clean, new ones. The third angel drew a special shape on his forehead, which marked him as belonging to the Prince. He also gave him a bright, golden key, called the key of promise, and a scroll which he was to keep on reading. He put the key and scroll in an inside pocket and the angels disappeared.

Christian was so happy that he couldn't keep still or quiet a moment longer, so he started jumping for joy and singing at the top of his voice. But he couldn't stay on the hilltop for ever, so he went happily on his way, walking down the hill and then along the valley at the bottom. Sometimes he chatted to other travellers, but most of the time he read his scroll as he travelled along. The words he read gave him hope and courage – both of which he was to need very soon.

At the valley's end lay a very steep hill called the Hill of Difficulty. The straight, narrow path ran right up to its side. Christian stopped to have a drink from a spring before tackling the slope.

At first he made good progress and encouraged himself with the words: 'Better the right way, though hard, than the wrong one, though easy'. But after a while, the slope became steeper and the path rockier, so he was forced to clamber up on his hands and knees.

Halfway up the hill, he came across a shady place in which a bench had been put. Here he sat down to rest and to read from his scroll. Little by little, his eyelids drooped lower and lower and finally he fell fast asleep. His hands relaxed and the scroll slipped on to the ground and then rolled under the seat.

The sun moved lower and lower in the sky and still he slept on.

Interpreter

Interpreter was a born teacher. He was clever, imaginative, good at explaining things and never boring! Christian might have found himself in all sorts of trouble if he had not spent some time at Interpreter's amazing house, talking to this wise man and finding out more about the way ahead.

It's possible that when John Bunyan created the character he called Interpreter, he was thinking of what Jesus said in the Bible in John chapter 14 verse 26: 'The Helper, the Holy Spirit...will teach you everything and make you remember all that I have told you'.

Think about it

It is Jesus Christ who died on the cross to save sinners. Do you realise that you are a sinner? But if you trust in Jesus Christ you will be forgiven. What does it feel like to be forgiven? Is it easy to forgive others?

Bible Search

All sinners need to be forgiven by God if they are to receive eternal life. Find out what the Bible says about forgiveness:

Psalm 32:1

Luke 6:37

Luke 17:3

Acts 13:38

Hebrews 8:12

1 John 1:9

The Fight

'Wake up, Lazy-bones!' said a voice, and Christian
woke with a guilty start and looked around. There was
no one to be seen.

'I must have slept for hours,' he thought, noticing
the afternoon shadows which had fallen over the hill.
He jumped up and went on with his climb. Before he
reached the top, he saw two men running down the
hill, so he shouted to them, 'Hey, you're going the
wrong way!'

'If you mean the wrong way for heaven, you're
right,' panted one of them, named Timorous. 'We *were*

on our way there, but the farther we went, the harder things got, and now we have had enough and are going home.'

'That's right,' agreed the other, called Mistrust. 'Seeing those lions was the last straw. We weren't going to risk being mauled to death by them, thank you very much!'

Some of the fear which Timorous and Mistrust felt rubbed off on to Christian, but he said, 'Going back home would be asking for certain death, so I'm going on, even though I'm scared, too. At my journey's end, lie heaven and safety.'

'Suit yourself!' said Timorous, and he and his companion hurried down the hill, while Christian kept on climbing to the top. He was badly in need of comfort and courage, so he felt in his pocket for his scroll. It wasn't there! Horrified, he stood still, wondering what could have happened. The last time he remembered reading the scroll was just before he had fallen asleep, so the only thing to do was to turn round and go back.

Poor Christian went sadly and slowly downhill, looking anxiously at the ground all the way, but it was no use. By the time he reached the resting-place he felt desperate, and sat down on the bench to have a good cry. Then he noticed something under the seat, and bent down to take a closer look. It was his precious scroll!

Eagerly he picked it up and put it away, thanking God for helping him to find it. Then, for the second time that day, he climbed towards the hilltop. Before he reached it, the sun set and darkness fell. How he wished he had not wasted hours of daylight in sleep! Then he thought of Timorous, Mistrust and the lions, and nearly panicked.

It was a relief to see, just then, a large building ahead and Christian went towards it, hoping to find a room for the night there.

This place was Palace Beautiful and in front of it was the gatekeeper's cottage. A narrow path led to the cottage and Christian set off along it. Suddenly he stopped dead in his tracks, his heart beating fast.

Just ahead of him crouched two lions, one on either side of the path. They looked huge, hungry and ferocious. Christian was about to turn tail and run, when a voice called out, 'Don't be afraid! The lions are chained and won't hurt you, if you walk in the middle of the path. Trust me – and come!'

Christian's legs were shaking, but he obeyed. The lions roared as he came closer but that was all, so he clapped his hands boldly and hurried straight past them.

When he reached the gate, Watchful, the gatekeeper, who had called out to him at just the right moment, let him in. Christian explained who he was and why he had arrived at such a late hour and asked whether he could stay for the night.

'I'll have to ask one of the caretakers of the big house,' was the reply from Watchful, as he pulled on a rope. From the direction of the main building came the muffled sound of a bell. A moment later, a young girl came walking gracefully towards them. Her name was Discretion, and she asked Christian a few questions about himself, before calling her sisters, Piety, Prudence and Charity. They came and spoke to Christian, too.

After a brief conversation, the girls seemed satisfied that Christian was what he claimed to be — a traveller on the way to heaven. So they led him to the main house, opened the front door and said, 'Come in! This palace was built by the Lord of the Hill for pilgrims like yourself.'

Christian went thankfully inside and was soon enjoying a meal and talking to the girls. They told him more about the Lord of the Hill, who owned the palace.

'He fought and killed our great enemy who had the power of death,' they said. 'He had to leave the glory of heaven and die on a cross. But he did it all for love of pilgrims like yourself.' The sisters continued,

'Some of this household have seen him since his death, and heard him say how much he loves pilgrims. In fact, he has already made some of them into heavenly princes.'

After the meal, the girls showed him to a bedroom named Peace.

Charity

Christian was feeling very weak by the time he reached the home of Charity and her three sisters. The girls made him very welcome. They gave him the care, advice and help he needed. By the time he left, he felt ready for anything – or so he thought.

The writer of the story probably thought of Charity as being like the person described in the Bible in 1 Corinthians 13 verses 4 to 8. In these verses, new translations of the Bible use the world 'love', but older ones used 'charity'.

Think about it:

Christian was annoyed
and disapointed when
he lost his scroll. He
was very glad when he
found it once again but he wished that he
hadn't wasted so much time sleeping. What
things do you do which are a waste of time?
What things should we do instead?

Bible Search:

In the story the girls in
the Palace Beautiful tell
Christian how The Lord Jesus
Christ loves pilgrims. Look
up these verses to find out about God's love.

Psalm 145:8	Lamentations 3:22
John 3:16	John 15:9
John 15:13	Romans 5:8
Romans 8:39	Ephesians 5:1
Titus 3:4	1 John 3:1
1 John 3:16	1 John 4:8

The Battle with Apollyon

Christian woke up after a good night's sleep there, feeling so happy that he burst out singing.

He stayed in Palace Beautiful for a few days, exploring the rooms, which held many beautiful and interesting objects, and talking with the sisters.

One morning, the girls took him to the palace roof and pointed out, in the distance, the Delectable Mountains and the woods and waters of Immanuel's Land. The sight of them made Christian long to be on his way. So did a report from Watchful, the gatekeeper. He described a man whom he had seen passing the gates and following the straight and narrow path. Christian felt sure that he knew this person and became very excited at the thought of travelling with him. But first he had to be made ready for the journey.

The sisters fitted him with armour from head to foot and went with him as far as the bottom of the hill. There, they gave him some food and said goodbye. He thanked them very much, and then went on his way, striding across the valley below the hill. It was called the Valley of Humbling, and Christian was soon to find out why.

He had not gone far, before he saw an evil-looking beast coming towards him. His body was scaly and huge wings were folded across his back. His head was like a lion's, and his feet like a bear's. Fire and smoke were pouring out of his belly.

This could be none other than the demon-prince, Apollyon, a deadly enemy of the Prince to whom Christian belonged.

'Where have you come from?' growled the fiend.

'From the City of Destruction,' answered Christian, feeling very frightened, but determined not to run away.

'Then you are mine!' was the reply.

'Not any longer,' Christian answered bravely. 'Serving you brought me nothing but misery, and your wages are death.'

Apollyon thought he had better try a different approach, so he put on a friendly voice and said, 'Go home, and I'll see what can be done to improve things.'

'Oh, no!' Christian replied. 'I have promised to serve another Prince, the greatest one of all.'

'Then you'll come to grief. All his servants do!' the other warned.

'It looks that way, sometimes,' said Christian, 'but it isn't so, for in the end, all the Prince's subjects will share his glory.'

'Huh – and do you really think he'll welcome *you*?!' sneered the demon. '*You* – who tried to get rid of your burden another way, who slept on the hill and lost your scroll? *You* – who almost ran at the sight of the lions and who are out for your own glory?'

'You're right about all that,' admitted Christian.

'And there are other things you could have mentioned. But I was really sorry for all the wrong things I did, so I asked my Prince to forgive me – *and he did!*'

That was enough for Apollyon. He stopped pretending to be reasonable and stormed, 'I hate your Prince and all his laws and subjects. And I have come to fight you!'

'Then you'd better watch out!' Christian answered boldly. 'For I am on the King's highway, the way of holiness.'

'You don't scare me!' roared Apollyon. 'In fact, I swear I'll kill you before you take another step!' As he said this, he hurled a burning arrow at Christian, who fended it off with his shield.

There followed a desperate fight which lasted for hour after hour. First, Apollyon peppered his opponent with fiery arrows. Christian did his best to protect himself from these while using his double-bladed sword; even so, he was wounded in three places where his armour could not protect him – his head, hand and foot.

He fought on, but it was clear that he was growing weaker all the time. His enemy saw this and so rushed in close and began to wrestle with him, finally succeeding in bringing him crashing down. As Christian hit the ground, his sword flew out of his hand. Apollyon promptly pinned him to the earth so firmly that the pilgrim was hardly able to breathe.

'I've got you now!' gloated the monster, and raised his arm ready to deal his enemy a death-blow. But it never fell, for Christian, summoning up the last of his strength, reached out to grasp his sword, and plunged it into Apollyon's side, shouting, 'Oh, no, you haven't – not yet!'

The sword cut deep into the monster's flesh and he fell back as though badly wounded, so Christian thrust his blade in again, with the words, 'My Prince will give me victory over you!' This was too much for the demon-prince. He spread his wings and flew up into the air and out of sight.

Christian got shakily to his feet. He was weak and wounded, but happy and he thanked God for helping him to win.

Suddenly, a hand appeared, holding some leaves. 'These must be from the tree of life,' thought Christian, and he took them and held them over his wounds, which healed instantly. Then he brought out the food and drink the beautiful sisters had given him. Never had he enjoyed a meal so much!

He was now ready to face the rest of the valley, so he set off, with his sword in his hand, drawn and ready for use at any moment. But he reached the valley's end in safety - only to find himself in even greater danger.

Apollyon

Apollyon was the enemy of God, out to stop those who walked along God's way to the Heavenly City. He could change shape and when Christian met him he was disguised as a dragon. He tried to persuade Christian to return to his home town, which was part of Apollyon's kingdom. When Christian refused, the fiend attacked him.

John Bunyan chose the name of this evil person from the Bible – in Revelation chapter 9 verse 11. Another of his names comes in James chapter 4 verse 7. Look them up!

Think about it:

When you do something wrong do you sometimes have a horrible guilty feeling? The Bible tells us to take our sin and guilt to God and ask him for forgiveness. When the Devil tries to remind you of all the bad things you've done he will try and make you feel guilty again - but you can tell him that you've already been forgiven by God the Father!

Bible Search:

The Bible tells us that our lives are a battle between good and evil. But if we trust in God he will help us.

Look up these Bible verses to find out how.

Exodus 14:14   Deuteronomy 1:30

Psalm 35:1   2 Corinthians 10:4

1 Timothy 6:11-13

The Valley of Shadow

Christian's path ran straight ahead through another valley. He was just walking towards it when he met two men running out of the valley's mouth as though a pack of hounds were after them.

'Where are you going?' Christian called out to them. They slowed down when they were near enough to speak to him and panted, 'Back – that's where we're going, and you'll do the same if you have any sense.'

'Why?' asked Christian.

'Because of that valley – that's why! No wonder it's called the Valley of the Shadow of Death! You wouldn't believe what we saw and heard when we reached the entrance!' said one man.

'Well, what *did* you see and hear?' asked Christian.

'The noise was dreadful,' answered the other. 'Yelling and howling, as though people were being tortured all the time!'

'And goblins and satyrs and dragons all moving about in the pitch darkness!' added his companion.

Christian wondered how he'd managed to see these creatures in the dark, but all he said was, 'You haven't convinced me that I'm going the wrong way.'

'That's up to you,' said the men. 'We'll be off, anyway.'

So they hurried away while Christian went forward towards the valley, holding his drawn sword in front of him all the time.

He reached the entrance and peered ahead. Clearly, the two frightened men had not exaggerated the dangers of the valley!

The place was very dark and his path, as far as he could see it, was extremely narrow and had swampy ground on one side of it and a deep ditch on the other.

Christian groped his way forward, step by step, for a good distance. Then he saw something which rooted him to the spot.

Just ahead, flames and smoke were pouring out of what appeared to be a vast hole.

'I must be standing at the mouth of hell,' he thought, his knees knocking together and his heart pounding. Showers of sparks from the fire kept falling on him, while weird and frightening noises from all around convinced him that hideous and frightful creatures were lurking close by. Against these dangers, his sword was no use, so he put it away and used another weapon – prayer.

'Save me, dear Prince,' he cried out, and felt brave enough to inch forward, although he was still very frightened – and with good reason! The flames were crackling and leaping towards him, while cries of agony splintered the darkness all around. At the same time, unseen beings were rushing to and fro and he kept expecting them to tear him apart or trample over him. Yet he managed to keep going for several miles.

But then he heard a dreadful din.

It sounded as though a pack of fiends were coming straight for him! He was so terrified, that he couldn't move and didn't know what to do. For a second or two, he even wondered whether to turn round and go back, but he soon realised that this might be even more dangerous than going on. So he made up his mind to walk straight ahead.

All this time, the fiends had been coming nearer and nearer. When they were almost on top of him, Christian shouted, 'I will go on in God's strength.' This brought the demons to a sudden stop – just in time!

So Christian went on his way, and before he had gone far, he heard something very encouraging.

It was a voice ahead of him in the dark, saying, 'Though I walk through the Valley of the Shadow of Death, I will not be afraid of any evil, for you are with me.'

To hear the voice of another pilgrim reminding him that God was not far away was just what Christian needed to help him walk quickly through the rest of the valley.

The sun rose, as he came out into the daylight, feeling very relieved. Just for a moment, he stopped to look back. When he saw by the morning's light the dangers he had come through, he felt very grateful for his escape.

Then he turned round and saw what lay ahead – the second half of the Valley of the Shadow of Death! It came as quite a shock to Christian to realise that he had only come through the first half! The way ahead looked, if anything, more dangerous than the way he had left behind. The ground was uneven and strewn with all sorts of traps and pitfalls. He dreaded to think what might have happened if he had had to get past them in the dark. As it was, he stepped out boldly, and managed to avoid every obstacle. So he reached the end of the valley without coming to any harm.

And then he saw ahead of him the man he had been trying to catch up with ever since he had left the Palace Beautiful. Just as he'd thought – it was Faithful, an old friend from the City of Destruction!

'Hey, wait for me!' Christian shouted, but Faithful was far too anxious to get right away from the valley to stop for anyone. So Christian ran to try and catch up with him. He not only caught up with his friend, he also overtook him – and this made him feel rather proud of himself. But the next moment, he tripped and fell.

Faithful hurried to his side and helped him up. Christian was unharmed. Only his pride had been dented, and he was so pleased to see Faithful that he quickly forgot about that!

The two travellers hugged each other, and walked on. Now that they were together, the journey seemed less tiring and the time passed by more quickly, as they talked happily and excitedly of their adventures. Having the same Prince and the same destination, made them feel like brothers.

'Did you fall into the Slough of Despond, Faithful?' asked Christian.

'No, but did *you* meet the woman called Wanton?' countered Faithful.

'No. What was she like?'

'The most beautiful woman you've ever seen! She did her best to get me off the right path, and almost succeeded, I'm afraid. The only way I managed to get past her was by shutting my eyes and running!'

'I'm not surprised,' remarked Christian. 'But what about the Hill of Difficulty? Did you climb that?'

'Eventually,' said Faithful, 'but only after a nasty encounter with Adam-the-first.'

'Oh, I never met him,' said Christian.

'Well, lucky for you!' exclaimed Faithful. 'He met me at the bottom of the hill and offered me a fantastic job. He said he was very rich and had a beautiful house and three gorgeous daughters, called Lust-of-the-flesh, Lust-of-the-eyes and Pride-of-life. If I worked for him, he said, I could marry all of them and then inherit everything when he died!'

'What did you say to all that?' asked Christian agog.

'Well, I was tempted to accept,' answered Faithful. 'After all he was a very old man and it sounded as if I had nothing to lose and everything to gain by taking the job. And then I noticed on his forehead the words: "Don't listen to the old man." That was enough for me.

But when I told him I didn't want anything from him – you should have seen his face. He was furious and said he'd send someone to beat me up. Then, when I turned to go, he pinched me so hard I thought he'd drawn blood. Anyway, I left him and started climbing the hill. But I soon realised that someone was following me. I did my best to shake him off but he caught up with me at the resting-place half-way up.'

'That's where I went to sleep and lost my scroll!' Christian exclaimed.

'Oh, really, but just listen to what happened to *me* there!' said Faithful. 'The man knocked me down – just like that! I passed out, I think, and when I came round I asked him why he'd hit me. He said, "Because you were tempted to go with Adam-the-first," and promptly punched me again! When I regained consciousness, I begged for mercy, but he said he didn't know the meaning of the word, and knocked me flat a third time. Perhaps he would have gone on to kill me, if someone else hadn't arrived at that moment and stopped him.'

'Oh, who was that?' asked Christian.

'I wasn't sure at first, but after he'd sent my attacker away and was about to leave, I noticed the scars on his hands and knew he was our Prince,' answered Faithful.

'The man who beat you up must have been Moses,' commented Christian. 'He can only *punish* those who break the law; he can't actually *help* them.'

'That's right,' said Faithful. 'I recognised him as soon as I saw him properly, because he was the one who made me leave home and start on this journey. In fact, he came to visit me one day, and threatened to burn my house down if I didn't leave at once – so I did. You'd already left, so I had to travel alone – till we met.'

'Didn't you notice the palace at the top of the hill?' asked Christian. 'The porter saw you walking straight past and told me about it. That's how I knew you were ahead of me.'

'Oh, I noticed it, all right,' replied Faithful. '*And* the lions, though they were asleep, I think. But I decided to go on, since the day was young and I could cover a lot of ground before nightfall.'

'I wish you could have stayed and seen some of the lovely things in Palace Beautiful,' said Christian. 'But tell me – did you meet anyone in the Valley of Humbling?'

'Yes, I met Discontent, who tried to make me turn back by telling me I'd gain nothing and lose all my friends by staying in that valley.'

'What did you say to that?'

'I told him that my so-called friends had disowned me the moment I'd decided to become a pilgrim and that anything I might gain by leaving the valley was nothing compared with the honours and joy of heaven.'

'And who else did you meet there?' Christian asked.

'A man called Shame, who did his best to make me feel ashamed of what I believed, the way I behaved and the people I mixed with. "Crying over your sins and asking people to forgive you for every little thing are unmanly things to do," he said. And I almost believed him, but then I asked myself: "Which is more important: what *people* think or what *God* thinks?" And of course, I knew the answer to that! God's wisdom is true wisdom.

There is no need to be ashamed of obeying *his* laws or mixing with *his* people. So I told Shame this and eventually managed to shake him off.'

'And a good thing too! But are you sure you didn't meet anyone else in the valley?'

'Quite sure,' replied Faithful. 'After that it was sunshine all the way.'

'Well, just you listen while I tell you who *I* met in the valley!' said Christian, who'd been bursting to tell this part of his story. Then he described vividly his battle with Apollyon, and his companion listened in amazement.

When they had finished telling each other their adventures, Faithful did something on the spur of the moment, which he later regretted.

Faithful

Faithful was the kind of person who stayed true to what he believed and to his friends, no matter what happened. He was a wonderful friend to Christian during the difficult times on their journey. Faithful was a good and loyal friend even to the very end.

John Bunyan may well have had Revelation chapter 2 verse 10 in mind when he wrote Faithful's part in the story. You might like to look it up in your Bible and find out why.

Think about it:

In the Valley of the Shadow Faithful says that he will fear no evil because God is with him. Think about the different situations you find yourself in when you get worried and scared. Would you find it helpful to know that God was with you? How might that help?

Bible Search:

God is with those who trust in him and there will come a time when his people will always be with him. Look up these Bible verses to find out where the Bible says that is:

Deuteronomy 31:6   Zephaniah 3:17
Matthew 28:20   Revelation 21:3

Vanity Fair

A handsome man had been walking along on the other side of the road for some time. Faithful now went over to him and asked, in a friendly way, whether they might walk and talk together for a while.

'Delighted!' the man replied. 'I like nothing better than to talk about important things, such as prayer and faith, suffering and truth, Christ and the good news of the gospel.'

Faithful was most impressed.

'Good!' he said. 'What shall we talk about?'

'Oh, anything you like,' said the man. 'Heaven or earth, past, present or future, big or small matters – you name it, I can talk about it!'

Faithful wasn't so sure he liked the sound of that, but he still thought the man would make a good travelling companion and went and told Christian so. But his friend smiled rather sadly and shook his head.

'I'm afraid you've been taken in,' he said. 'I know that man. He's Talkative, son of Saywell and lives in our town – in Prating-row, in fact. You haven't missed anything by not meeting him, I assure you! He's all talk and no action. He says all the right things, but his life is a mess!'

'Oh, dear!' said Faithful. 'How am I going to shake him off?'

'Just go and ask him about God's power to change a person's behaviour,' suggested Christian.

So Faithful walked across to Talkative again and asked him, 'What would you say happens when God starts working in a person's life?'

'First of all,' said Talkative, 'the person will speak out against all sin and wrong-doing.'

'But lots of people *speak out* against sin without actually *doing* anything about the things that are wrong in their own lives!' Faithful objected, adding, 'Do go on, though.'

'Secondly,' continued Talkative, sounding a little annoyed, 'a person will know a great deal about Christ and the good news.'

'*Knowing* about Jesus and *obeying* him are very different,' Faithful pointed out, at which Talkative, looking very cross, said, 'You're trying to catch me out – so I won't say another word!'

'May I go on then, please?' Faithful asked politely.

'No one's stopping you!' said Talkative coldly.

'Well, when God is at work in someone's life,' said Faithful, 'he begins to hate wrong and then he turns away from it and asks Christ to forgive him. The moment he trusts Christ, he begins a new life in which he wants to please his Saviour.'

Faithful paused, then looked pointedly at Talkative and asked, 'Have you put your trust in Christ? Are you telling others of your faith in him? Does the way you live agree with what you say?'

An angry flush now coloured Talkative's cheeks and he stalked off, saying, 'I don't wish to discuss these things!'

'I thought that would happen,' said Christian gently, coming over to Faithful's side.

'Anyway, I'm glad I had a talk with him,' said Faithful.

The two men went on walking and talking, so deep in conversation and so happy to be together that they hardly noticed the hot dusty ground over which they were now passing. At the end of this stretch of desert, they stopped to look back, and had a pleasant surprise. Coming up behind them was their old friend and guide – Evangelist. They waited for him to reach them.

'Peace to you!' Evangelist greeted them.

'And welcome to you!' they answered. Evangelist wanted to know how Christian and Faithful had been getting on since he had last met them, so they told him of their adventures.

'I'm so glad you kept to the right path, overcoming every difficulty,' Evangelist said. His face grew serious as he added, 'The going will get even harder, but stick to your road, no matter what you may meet.'

'Can you give us some idea of what to expect?' asked Christian.

'I can't tell you much,' replied Evangelist. 'But I know that just ahead lies a town. Its people will be out for your blood, and one of you will die.'

Christian and Faithful said goodbye to their friend and went on their way, thinking of Evangelist's words. They left the desert behind them and noticed a town not far ahead. It was called Vanity and was famous for its market, known as Vanity Fair. Here every kind of worthless pleasure was for sale, to tempt pilgrims from the path.

Christian and Faithful entered the town and began walking through its streets. But the townspeople quickly noticed the two strangers who dressed and spoke differently from everyone else and who showed no interest at all in any of the goods on sale in the market. They surrounded the pilgrims and began teasing and hitting them. Before long, the place was in an uproar.

The lord of the fair heard about this and ordered his servants to seize the two men and bring them before the magistrates immediately.

Christian and Faithful didn't defend themselves against the men who grabbed them and dragged them through the streets, but when they were face-to-face with the magistrates, they spoke up boldly for themselves.

'We're pilgrims on our way to the heavenly city, and have no wish to cause trouble,' they said, but it was no use.

'If you're not troublemakers, you're mad!' the magistrates told them. 'Either way, you deserve punishment.' Then they had the prisoners beaten and smeared with dirt and afterwards locked up in a cage, so that the townspeople could mock and insult them to their hearts' content.

All this time, Christian and Faithful behaved so quietly and graciously that a few bystanders were touched and impressed in spite of themselves, and tried to restrain the others. But their efforts only made matters worse and in the end a scuffle broke out between the two groups.

As a result, Christian and Faithful were taken from the cage and dragged off for a second trial. The magistrates put all the blame for the fight on to the pilgrims and their punishment was a cruel beating. Then iron bands were clamped to their wrists and ankles. Wearing these and trailing long chains, they had to walk through the streets which were lined with sneering people.

Again, Christian and Faithful bore everything so patiently and quietly that some of the onlookers were very moved – especially a young man named Hopeful. But the rest were so furious that they made up their minds to have the pilgrims killed. For the moment they put them back into the cage, locking their feet into wooden stocks.

In spite of everything, the prisoners didn't lose hope. Instead they comforted each other by remembering what Evangelist had said. Each secretly hoped he would be the one to die and so reach heaven first, but both prayed that God's will would be done, whatever happened.

Then they were taken for a third trial – this time before a judge and jury. The judge was an evil man named Lord Hategood, and his twelve jurymen were vicious rogues.

Lord Hategood opened the trial and the charge against the prisoners was read out: 'These men have disturbed our trade, caused trouble and won over several townspeople to their way of thinking, which is against the law of our prince.'

Faithful spoke up in reply to this charge.

'I am a man of peace,' he said. 'Those who want to join us do so of their own free will and because they saw the way we behaved. What's more, they are right to change loyalties, for the prince they serve is Beelzebub – and I defy him and all his angels.

From that moment, Faithful was treated as though he were the only one on trial.

'Is there a witness for the prosecution against the accused?' asked Lord Hategood.

'There is,' said a man, stepping forward. His name was Envy and he pointed at Faithful and said, 'That vile man says our laws are completely against Christianity!'

The next witness – Superstition by name – added, 'The prisoner says our worship is empty and meaningless!'

The third and last witness was called Pickthank – a man whose aim was to be nice to people in authority, hoping for favours in return.

'My Lord Judge, the man before you has said some very disrespectful things about our prince, Beelzebub, as well as about all the great men in our town,' he said, and proceeded to name them, so that everyone would think he knew these important people personally. Then he added, 'He has even, I regret to say, said some terrible things about *you*, your worship!'

That was enough for the judge. He turned on Faithful. 'You cowardly traitor!' he said. 'Have you heard what these good men have told us?'

'May I say a few words in my defence?' asked Faithful.

'You deserve to be killed on the spot,' answered the judge. 'But, just so that everyone will see how fair we are, let us hear what you have to say.'

'As far as the first witness is concerned,' Faithful began. 'I would like to point out that what I actually said was that *any* laws which don't agree with God's word are not Christian.'

Then he turned to the second witness and continued, 'All worship based on *human* faith is pointless and does not please God. True worship means understanding and obeying God's will.'

Faithful paused, then continued, 'In reply to the third witness, all I want to say is that your prince and all his followers are better suited to hell than to this place!'

By this time, Lord Hategood's eyes were blazing with hatred, but he pretended to sum up the proceedings fairly in a closing speech. He began by telling the jury to consider their verdict carefully, for they had the power to condemn or free the prisoner, but ended by saying that Faithful had admitted to treason and so deserved death.

The jury did not take long to reach a unanimous verdict: the prisoner was guilty and should be put to death – in the cruellest possible manner.

Talkative

Talkative seemed the ideal travelling companion – friendly, good-looking and a very good talker. That's what Faithful thought, but Christian knew better. He knew that the man said all the right things, but his behaviour was all wrong.

In creating Talkative's character, John Bunyan had the Bible verse in Matthew chapter 23 verse 3 in mind. Can you see the connection?

Lord Hategood

Lord Hategood was the opposite of what a judge should be. He hated right and loved wrong, because he did wrong himself. Christian and Faithful stood for what was right and were good, and so the judge hated the very sight of them and had already made up his mind that they would be found guilty.

Lord Hategood did the opposite of what God told people to do in the Bible in Amos chapter 5 verse 15: 'Hate what is evil, love what is right, and see that justice prevails in the courts'.

Think about it:

When Faithful was having a conversation with Talkative he told him that when God is working in someone's life that person changes. In what ways does that person change? Do you think you have changed in this way?

Bible Search:

We are told to trust in God. Look up the following verses to find out what the Bible says about that.

Psalm 9:10

Psalm 56:3

Isaiah 12:2

Romans 15:13

Psalm 20:7

Proverbs 3:5-6

John 14:1

A New Friend

The mockery of a trial was over. Faithful had been condemned to death by burning – but first he had to endure all kinds of torture. His enemies beat him and knocked him about; they threw stones and prodded him with their swords. Finally they tied him to a wooden post and set alight the sticks and logs which were piled around his feet and legs. The bonfire was soon ablaze.

As far as the townspeople were concerned, Faithful was burnt to ashes. They did not see him being swept up through the clouds and into heaven in a horse-drawn chariot.

Christian, meanwhile, had been flung into prison for the time being. But it was not God's plan that he should meet the same fate as Faithful, and so he escaped from there, with the help of a few of the people who had been impressed by the pilgrims.

Amongst these was Hopeful. He helped Christian get away from the prison and then asked whether he could join him in his journey.

Christian was only too pleased to agree, so the two men walked happily together along the King's Highway.

Before long they met and talked to four other travellers, but these proved to be false pilgrims and so Christian and Hopeful left them behind and walked on until they reached the Plain of Ease.

It wasn't a big place, so they crossed it quite easily, only stopping once, just before they left it. Here they paused to look to the left where there were some mine-workings at the bottom of a small hill, called Lucre. A man was standing nearby and he saw the travellers and called out, 'Come over here. I've got something to show you'.

'What exactly is this thing which you think we should go out of our way to see?' asked Christian cautiously.

'Why, a silver mine!' answered the man. 'Full of treasure which is yours for the taking!'

Hopeful was curious. 'Let's take a look,' he said, but Christian shook his head.

'I've heard of this place,' he said quietly and then called out to the stranger, 'Isn't the ground near the mine dangerous?'

'Not very,' he answered, but his cheeks flushed bright red as he spoke.

'Let's be on our way,' said Christian briskly to Hopeful, and the two men prepared to walk on.

'Aren't you even going to take a *look*?' shouted the man by the mine. Only then did Christian speak sharply.

'You're just trying to make us do what you did – step off the right way,' he said accusingly.

'Not at all!' protested the other. 'I'm one of you, and if you'll just wait a bit, I'll join you.'

'Hmm,' said the pilgrim suspiciously. 'Isn't your name Demas?'

'That's right!'

'Then I know exactly who you are!' exclaimed Christian. 'Your grandfather was greedy Gehazi and your father was Judas, the traitor, and you deserve his fate for trying to trick us into leaving the path!'

Demas was silenced at last, so the pilgrims walked quickly away.

They came next to a delightful place, with pleasant fields full of sweet-smelling lilies, and a sparkling river bordered by trees laden with luscious fruit.

Here they stayed for several days, eating the fruit for food, and the leaves for medicine, and drinking the water in the River of the Water of Life.

It would have been pleasant to stay here longer, but their journey wasn't over yet, and their path stretched out ahead of them.

They set off, feeling well and strong and fit for anything – or so they thought. But before long, the path led them further and further from the river, and deeper and deeper into rougher, stonier country, so that they grew tired and foot-sore. It was then that they caught a glimpse of a smooth, green meadow on the other side of a fence: By-path Meadow! How cool and inviting it looked!

'Let's just see if this field runs beside our path,' said Christian, and he went across to a stile in the fence to have a look. Sure enough, it did, so he said, 'Come on, Hopeful! There's a nice, smooth path running along just inside the fence – let's take it!'

'But what if it takes us out of our way?' asked Hopeful.

'Unlikely!' answered Christian. 'Look – can't you see that the two paths go the same way?' With these words, he climbed over the stile and into the meadow, and Hopeful followed.

The path there was certainly easier on their feet, and they were able to walk along more quickly. Not far ahead of them was a man, to whom Christian called out, 'Excuse me – where does this path go?'

'To the gate of the heavenly city,' the man called back.

'Told you so!' exclaimed Christian to Hopeful with a triumphant smile. And so, foolishly, they followed the stranger – not knowing that he was not to be trusted, since he merely hoped for the best, as his name – Vain-Confidence – suggested.

After a while, it grew dark and they could no longer see their guide. Then, suddenly, there was an echoing shout, followed by silence. Horrified, Christian and Hopeful groped their way towards the sound – only to find a deep hole yawning at their feet. They called down to the poor man who had evidently fallen into this but he did not reply, and all they could hear, from far below, were muffled groans.

'What are we going to do now?' asked Hopeful. Christian was silent, beginning to suspect that he had made a terrible mistake.

A thunderstorm suddenly blew up. The thunder and flashes of lightning were terrifying, and the rain was so heavy that the ground quickly flooded.

'Forgive me, brother, for leading you astray and into such danger!' Christian said.

'I *do* forgive you,' answered kind-hearted Hopeful.

'Let's get back to the stile,' Christian suggested. But the water was so high by this time that they were in danger of being swept off their feet and drowned, so they were forced to give up the attempt and had to shelter under a tree instead. Here, not knowing what a dangerous place they were in, they fell into an exhausted sleep.

The meadow was part of the grounds of Doubting Castle, owned by Giant Despair. Next morning, this terrible ogre caught sight of the sleeping pair and came across to shake them roughly awake, demanding, 'What are you doing on my land?'

'We're pilgrims who have lost our way,' blurted out poor Christian and Hopeful, hoping that they were still dreaming.

'Trespassers, more like!' roared the giant. 'But I've caught you red-handed, so come along with me!' As he said these words, he pulled the pilgrims to their feet and then drove them, with kicks and punches, towards his castle. Once there, he threw them down some steps and afterwards pushed them into a dark, stinking cell, where he locked them up.

Christian and Hopeful lay on the floor, half-stunned for a moment, but soon they realised how bad their situation was. They were prisoners in that grimmest of all prisons, Doubting Castle, and their warder was none other than Giant Despair, well-known for his savage cruelty – and for his wife, Diffidence.

Both men were overwhelmed by misery, but Christian was feeling guilty as well.

'It's all my fault!' he thought, despairingly. 'If only I hadn't left the path and persuaded Hopeful to follow me! *Now* what's going to happen to us?'

Hopeful

Hopeful just 'hoped for the best' before he became a pilgrim. Afterwards, he hoped in God, and so was full of confidence, knowing that God would never let him down. His cheerful trusting nature was a great help to Christian as the two pilgrims travelled on together.

The kind of hopefulness in Hopeful's character after he became a pilgrim was the sort mentioned in 1 Peter chapter 1 verse 13. Possibly John Bunyan had this verse in mind as he wrote about Hopeful. You might like to look up the verse in your Bible and see what you think.

Think about it:

Christian and Hopeful lost their way - how did that happen? Have you ever been lost? What did it feel like? Read this verse: Psalm 119:176 'I have strayed like a lost sheep. Seek your servant, for I have not forgotten your commands.' That verse describes all of us for we have all sinned. Now read Proverbs 8:17 'I love those who love me, and those who seek me find me.' This is God's promise and he always keeps his promises.

Bible Search:

God wants to rescue his people. Read the following verses to find out more about this.

Proverbs 8:17

Luke 15:5-7

Matthew 18:14

Luke 19:10

Doubting Castle

'Well, wife,' said Giant Despair, when he went to bed that night, 'I've caught two trespassers. So now, what shall I do with them?'

'Who are they?' asked Diffidence.

'They say they are pilgrims on their way to the heavenly city,' answered her husband.

An evil gleam came into his wife's eyes.

'Beat them, and make a good job of it,' she commanded.

'Just as you say, my dear,' he replied.

So, in the morning, he snatched up a vicious-looking wooden club and went down to the cell.

'Come here, you dogs,' he shouted and then rushed over and began beating Christian and Hopeful until they were a mass of bruises. Finally, he left them.

All that day they lay on the floor, too sore to move and groaning in agony.

'Well, my dear,' said the giant to his wife that night. 'What's to be done now?'

'Do you mean to say they are still alive?' snapped his wife.

'Well, yes, but only just,' her husband mumbled.

'Huh! Call yourself a giant and yet you can't even finish off a couple of puny pilgrims!' she jeered. Her husband looked sulky, but said nothing, so she went on, 'Right then, in the morning, go and tell them to kill themselves – for their own good, of course.' Then she added, with a malicious smirk, 'And let them choose their method: the knife, the rope or the poison!'

'What good ideas you have!' remarked the giant, in a voice oily with flattery.

The next morning, he went to the prisoners and told them very bluntly that their best course would be suicide.

'We wouldn't dream of doing such a thing. Please let us go,' answered Hopeful.

This reply infuriated the giant. His face twisted into a snarl and he lunged at the prisoners as though he would kill them on the spot, but something stopped him just in time.

The giant suffered from occasional fits and one gripped him just at that moment, making him incapable of moving for some time. Afterwards, he just had the strength to take himself off to his bed for a sleep.

All this had been too much for Christian. 'Let's kill ourselves and end this torture,' he said in black despair.

Hopeful shook his head firmly.

'That would be committing murder – which our Prince has forbidden us to do,' he pointed out. 'Besides,' he added, trying to sound as cheerful as possible, 'something might happen to help us get out of this place. Others have managed to escape, so why shouldn't we? God might make Giant Despair die. Or he might have another fit, and if he does, I'm determined to take the chance and try to get away. I only wish I'd thought of it before – when he was having a fit right here in our cell! But whatever happens, we mustn't disobey our Prince by committing murder.'

That evening, the giant, fully recovered from his illness, came back to the cell, expecting to find a couple of dead bodies. When he saw that the pilgrims had not obeyed him and were still alive, though only just, all his fury returned and he bellowed, 'You'll soon be wishing you'd never been born, or my name's not Giant Despair!' Then he stormed out.

Christian was at the end of his tether. For a moment or two he even fainted and when he came to, he repeated his suggestion that they should end their troubles by killing themselves, but Hopeful would not hear of it.

'Just think of the dangers you've come safely through!' he said encouragingly to Christian. 'Apollyon and the Valley of the Shadow of Death, to mention only two!'

Christian made no answer, so Hopeful continued, 'We're in the same boat, remember! We've both been beaten, starved and left in the dark for days on end, and I'm a much weaker person than you are, so if *I* can survive, *you* can, too! Think back to Vanity Fair – and how patient and brave you were there!'

Up in the giant's bedroom that night, it was Diffidence who broached the subject of the prisoners. 'Did they take your advice?' she asked her husband.

'No – they'll put up with anything rather than take their own lives,' he replied.

'Hmm, I wonder!' Diffidence muttered spitefully, as she turned over various nasty ideas in her mind. When she had chosen one, she said, 'I think I know how to make them change their minds! Show them the bones and skulls of the pilgrims you have already killed, and make them believe that you'll do the same to them – before the week's out!'

So, the very next morning, Giant Despair dragged Christian and Hopeful out of their cell, up the steps and into the courtyard. While the two men stared in horror at the human bones scattered over the ground, the giant passed on the threatening message his wife had thought up. The pilgrims were then punched and pummelled all the way back to their cell by their vicious warder.

That night the giant grumbled to his wife, 'Why haven't those dogs of pilgrims killed themselves? I can't understand it! I've done everything in my power to make them want to die!'

Diffidence couldn't understand it either, and was not at all pleased. So she thought very hard until she felt sure she had found the answer – and a very shrewd one it was, as things turned out.

'They must be nursing a secret hope,' she said. 'Either they're expecting someone to come and rescue them, or they're hiding a weapon capable of picking prison locks, and waiting for the right moment to use it.'

'How clever you are, my dear!' purred the giant, switching on a twisted smile. 'I'll search every inch of the cell and of their miserable bodies tomorrow morning,' he added.

That was his big mistake.

While the giant and his wife slept, strange things were happening in the cell far below. Hopeful had at last succeeded in putting a little spirit back into Christian and so, from midnight onwards, the two men did what they should have done in the first place – they prayed.

Just before dawn Christian leapt to his feet, exclaiming, 'What a fool I've been! What a complete and total idiot! All this time we could have been free, if only I'd remembered this!' And he pulled something out of an inner pocket and held it up.

It was a gleaming key – the key of promise. Hopeful's eyes sparkled.

'Let's try it, straight away!' he said. So they went to the cell door and Christian put the key into the keyhole and turned it. The lock flew open!

Eagerly the prisoners pushed open the door and hurried out of their cell, up the stairs and across a passage leading to the door into the courtyard. The key opened this door, too. They went quietly across the yard and over to the iron gate. This time the key was very stiff to turn, but eventually it did and the lock opened. Quickly they pushed at the big, heavy, iron gate. As it swung back, the hinges creaked noisily, but this only made the pilgrims run even faster across the meadow.

Giant Despair was woken from sleep by the creaking hinges and leapt out of bed, but that was as far as he got, for one of his fits came on just then and kept him out of action until Christian and Hopeful were safe on the King's Highway once more!

What a nightmare they had been through! And how thankful they were to be free at last! However, they took the time and trouble to set up a post near the stile and write something on it which they hoped would stop other travellers from straying into By-path Meadow. And this is what they wrote:

Over this stile is the way to Doubting Castle, kept by Giant Despair, who despises the Prince of the heavenly city and wants to destroy his pilgrims.

Afterwards, they went on their way, singing for sheer happiness at their miraculous escape. Perhaps if they had known what lay ahead, they might have sung about that, too!

Giant Despair

Giant Despair was a desperate and powerful ogre. He hated pilgrims and, when he managed to get them into one of his dungeons, did all he could to make them lose hope. Christian and Hopeful fell into his clutches one morning and were soon in torment.

Perhaps John Bunyan was thinking of what the Bible says in James chapter 1 verse 6 when he invented Giant Despair and Doubting Castle. Do you agree?

Think about it:

What was the name of Christian's special key? Can you remember when he received it? There are lots of promises in God's word. Someone once said that there is a promise for every day of the year - even on a leap year. Do you make promises? Do you find them easy or difficult to keep? God always keeps his promises. Isn't that amazing.

Bible Search:

We can trust God to keep his promises. Sometimes we might think he has forgotten but he hasn't. Look up the following verses:

2 Peter 3:9   Genesis 9:15

Isaiah 49:15   2 Peter 3:8

The Mountains

Christian and Hopeful arrived next at the Delectable Mountains, and found them just as delightful as their name suggested.

After a short climb, they came across beautiful gardens and rich vineyards of ripe grapes, all watered by sparkling fountains. Here the travellers stopped to admire the flowers, eat the grapes and wash their hands and feet.

Before going on, they made for themselves a couple of walking sticks which they thought they might need when climbing the steep, upper slopes.

These sticks were a help, but even so it was a tiring climb and they were not sorry to stop and rest near the top, where shepherds were watching their sheep. Leaning on his walking stick, Christian asked one of them, 'Could you tell me, please – who owns all this?'

'The mountains are part of Immanuel's land, which belongs to the Prince. The sheep are his, too, because he died for them,' the man replied. His voice was polite, but he looked hard at the pilgrims as he spoke.

'Are we on the right road for the heavenly city?' Christian asked next.

'You are.'

'Is the way ahead safe or dangerous?'

'Safe for some,' answered the shepherd. 'For others – those who keep doing wrong – it's dangerous.'

'Is there anywhere for tired travellers to rest?' Christian wanted to know.

'Of course,' was the friendly reply. 'The Prince wants us to be kind to strangers, so everything we have is yours if you need it. But tell me, please – where have you come from, and how did you get here?'

As the pilgrims answered these questions, all four shepherds gathered round to listen. When Christian and Hopeful had finished their story, the men smiled at them, held out their hands and said, 'Welcome to the Delectable Mountains!' They introduced themselves as Sincere, Watchful, Knowledge and Experience.

Then they took Christian and Hopeful over to their tents and gave them food and drink. As they were talking together afterwards, Experience said, 'We would like you to spend a few days with us before you go on, for we want to show you some places around here.'

The pilgrims were glad to accept this invitation. In the next few days, they were shown some frightening sights and they learnt many things from these and from their talks with the shepherds.

One of these sights was a precipice known as the Hill of Error. The shepherds told Christian and Hopeful that some pilgrims had strayed from the path and had fallen straight down this. It was not a pleasant thought.

On another day they all climbed a peak known as Mount Caution. From here they were able to make out in the distance some men in a graveyard. They were fumbling about, as though in the dark, groping from one tombstone to another and apparently unable to find their way out of the place.

'These men were captured and blinded by Giant Despair,' said Knowledge – and Christian and Hopeful exchanged horrified looks but said nothing. 'Afterwards,' continued the shepherd, 'he took them to that graveyard and left them. They've been wandering about there ever since, trying to find a way out, but never succeeding.'

This sad story brought tears to the pilgrims' eyes, but they still said nothing about their own terrifying stay with the grim giant.

The next day the shepherds showed them something even more spine-chilling. In the middle of a hillside lay a door. Sincere grasped the handle and opened it, saying, 'Look in there!'

Christian and Hopeful saw a huge black hole and peered cautiously down it – but what they saw and heard was almost too much for them, and after a brief look, they were shaking from head to foot.

The hole was the entrance to a tunnel at the bottom of which, judging by a roaring sound and billowing smoke, was an immense fire. Most terrifying of all were the agonised shrieks and cries of people in torment, which they could hear from far below.

The pilgrims drew back, their faces pale.

'What is that place?' asked Christian, shakily.

'A by-way to hell,' said Knowledge. 'It's the path chosen by liars and cheats and those who sell their souls for money.'

'So it's possible to turn away from the right path and be lost for ever, even after getting this far!' murmured Christian in horror.

'Yes, and even further,' answered Experience.

By this time, Hopeful and Christian were eager to be on their way again, so the shepherds escorted them over the mountains for some distance.

Then Watchful looked round at his friends and said, 'Let's show them the gates of the heavenly city!' They agreed, so Christian and Hopeful were taken up a nearby hill called Clear, and told to look through a special telescope in a certain direction.

Their hands were still shaking from the shock of seeing Hell's By-way and so they couldn't hold the telescope completely steady. This meant that the picture wasn't as clear as it might have been, but even so they were able to catch a glimpse of some gates with bright light all round them. This sight was just the boost they needed to send them happily on their way again. But first each of the shepherds had some final words for them.

Knowledge said, 'Here are your directions to the heavenly city,' and handed Christian some paper with writing on it.

'Beware of the Flatterer,' Watchful said.

Experience added, 'And whatever you do, don't go to sleep on the Enchanted Ground.' Last of all Sincere smiled and wished them 'Godspeed'.

Christian and Hopeful thanked their kind hosts and then set off down the mountain, singing as they went.

At the bottom, their path was smooth and level for some distance and they followed it, without difficulty. Then they came to the lane.

It was very small and dark, but their way lay straight through it.

'Come on, Hopeful,' said Christian. 'We mustn't stop, whatever happens. I know a true story about a man who slept at the entrance to this lane – and afterwards wished with all his heart he hadn't!'

So Hopeful walked bravely along beside Christian, who went on with his story.

'The man I was telling you about,' he said, 'was called Little-faith, from the Town of Sincere. And, as I said, he slept in this lane. Well, when he had woken up and was about to move on, he heard shouts of, "Stop, or we'll *make* you!" So he stopped and turned round.

'There stood three villains whom he knew by sight and by name as Mistrust, Guilt, and Faint-heart. They looked most unfriendly, and Guilt was grasping a vicious-looking stick. Poor Little-faith went as white as a sheet and stood there – too scared to fight or run.

'"Hand over your money!" hissed Faint-heart. Naturally, Little-faith hesitated, so Mistrust rushed over, plunged a hand in his pocket and pulled out a fistful of silver coins.

'Then at last Little-faith found his voice and shouted, "Thieves! Thieves!" But Guilt promptly silenced him, by flattening him with one blow on the head from his cudgel.

'Just then, footsteps and voices could be heard approaching, so the three rogues took to their heels, leaving Little-faith unconscious and bleeding badly. Eventually, he came round and managed to get up and stagger further down the lane.'

'How awful!' exclaimed Hopeful. 'Did the thieves rob him of everything?'

'Well, they left him with very little money, so he had to beg for his food after that, but, surprisingly, they didn't manage to steal his jewels or his scroll!'

'He must have been pleased about the jewels, at least!' said Hopeful.

'You'd have thought so!' answered Christian. 'But I'm told that the poor man never really recovered from his experience, and couldn't talk or think of anything after that – except the terrible time he had had!'

Hopeful felt that Little-faith had been cowardly and lacking in spirit from start to finish of this sad story, and he said as much to Christian, who did not agree.

'If you had actually met these villains, and their master, the King of the Bottomless Pit, as I did once, you wouldn't be quite so ready to blame Little-faith,' he retorted.

Hopeful at first felt a little nettled at being put in his place like that, but it wasn't long before he admitted that Christian was in the right and was his old cheerful self again.

And then they came to the fork in the road.

Knowledge

Knowledge was wise, thoughtful and studious. He had learnt many things about God and his way, which he was anxious to pass on to others. Christian and Hopeful discovered many new truths from him and from his three fellow-shepherds in the Delectable Mountains.

Perhaps the writer of this story got the idea of calling one of the shepherds Knowledge from a Bible verse found in Colossians chapter 1 verse 9.

Think about it:

Christian and Hopeful were given warnings. They were scared by some of these warnings. When is it a good thing to be scared? How can it help you and even save your life?

Bible Search:

Here are some warnings from God. You would do well to pay attention to them so look these verses up in the Bible:

Deuteronomy 5:32   Deuteronomy 11:16
Joshua 1:7   Matthew 6:1
1 Corinthians 10:12   Hebrews 2:1

A Testing Time

'Which way do we go now?' asked Hopeful, for both paths ahead looked straight.

'I'm not sure,' answered Christian. As the pilgrims stood there hesitating, a dark man dressed in white came across to them and said, 'Can I help you?'

'We're on our way to the heavenly city,' Christian explained to the stranger, 'but we don't know which road to take.'

'I'm going in your direction,' the man replied. 'Follow me.' And he set off along one of the paths. Christian and Hopeful followed.

It seemed the natural thing to do, and besides, it was rather flattering to have a guide all to themselves.

The road they were walking along gradually veered away from the direction in which they had been travelling, until they almost had their backs to the heavenly city. Yet they still followed the stranger, and all went well, for a time. Then suddenly a net fell on top of Christian and Hopeful and quickly closed round them, as their guide hurried away. Too late, they realised that they had walked straight into a trap and that their so-called guide was the Flatterer!

'If only we'd remembered what Watchful said!' sighed Christian.

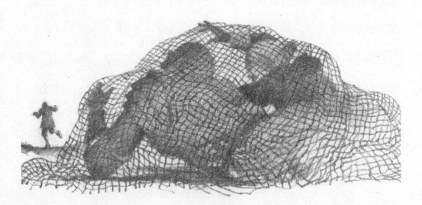

'Or looked at the directions which Knowledge gave us,' added Hopeful.

His companion was too busy struggling to free himself from the rope to take the paper out of his pocket, but he was sure that it would only tell him what he already knew – that they were on the wrong path!

The two men tugged and strained at the ropes, but it was no use. They were worn out and ready to cry with frustration, when they saw someone approaching.

It was an angel. He came straight up to the net and asked, 'What *are* you doing in there?' The pilgrims told him about the fork in the road and the guide they had followed. Without another word, the angel bent down and picked up part of the net. Then he simply tore a large hole in it, snapping the ropes as easily as if they were threads, and the pilgrims stepped out – very thankful to be free.

'Follow me,' said the angel, and he turned and walked back. The two men followed and were soon standing on the King's Highway again. Here the angel stopped, looked them straight in the eyes and asked them, 'Where were you last night?'

'With the shepherds on the Delectable Mountains,' answered Christian.

'Didn't they give you directions?' asked the angel.

'Yes, they did,' replied Christian and Hopeful, looking a little ashamed.

Then the angel asked, 'When you came to the fork in the road, didn't you even look at the instructions?'

'No, we forgot,' said Hopeful in a low voice.

The angel had one final question.

'Didn't the shepherds warn you about the Flatterer?' he asked.

'Yes, they did,' replied Christian, 'but we never thought he'd be as well-spoken as the man we met!'

By this time, the angel's face was both sad and stern, and he now said, 'I'm afraid that since you didn't learn by being *told* what to do, I shall have to *punish* you – and see whether that will teach you to listen and obey better in future.' Then he gave the pilgrims a good whipping. It hurt, but neither of them felt resentful, because each knew he deserved it and hoped it would do him good.

Afterwards, they thanked the angel for coming to help them, and then, wiser though sadder, went on their way. They even made up a song about their recent experience, and sang this as they walked along.

In this frame of mind, they made good progress. Then, looking ahead, they saw a man coming towards them. They did not know that his name was Atheist, but as the man came closer, Hopeful muttered to Christian, 'Be careful! He might be another flatterer.'

When Atheist was face-to-face with Christian and Hopeful he stopped and spoke to them.

'Where are you going?' he asked.

'To heaven,' said Hopeful. This reply seemed to amuse Atheist very much, for he threw back his head and laughed.

'What are you laughing at?' Christian wanted to know.

'I'm laughing at you – for being so simple,' Atheist said. 'You're on a wild-goose chase. There's no such place as heaven in this world!'

'But there is, in the *next world!*' retorted Christian.

'I used to believe that,' answered Atheist. 'But not anymore – and I should know! After all, I've been a globe-trotter for the past twenty years and in all that time I've never once seen any such place. Now I'm on my way home, to have a good time and catch up on all the fun I missed on this pointless journey!'

Christian looked at Hopeful and asked in a low voice, 'Do you think the man's right?'

'Watch out – he's one of the flatterers!' answered Hopeful, warningly. Then he added firmly, 'No heaven, indeed! Don't you remember the gates we saw from the Delectable Mountains? And haven't we been told by our Prince to travel in faith? Come on, Christian, let's be on our way. I certainly don't want another whipping!'

Hopeful's words brought a smile to Christian's face and his eyes twinkled as he said, 'Forgive me, brother, I was just testing you. I didn't really believe a word the man said. The god of this world has blinded his eyes, poor fellow. But we know that what we believe is true, so let's do as you say and walk on as fast as possible.'

'With our hope to keep us happy!' added Hopeful.

So the pilgrims walked on and Atheist continued with his journey home, laughing loud and long at the two men as he went. Ignoring him, they kept going – not knowing that a test of a different sort lay ahead.

The moment they reached the next place, they sensed that there was something strange in the air. It made them feel heavy-footed and very drowsy.

Hopeful said, 'Let's stop here and have a nap,' and then yawned several times.

'Not on your life!' said Christian, stifling a yawn.

Hopeful looked at him in amazement and said, 'Why not? Sleep is good!'

'Not here, not now,' answered Christian firmly. 'Come on, Hopeful! Don't you remember what Experience said about not sleeping on the Enchanted Ground?'

'So that's where we are!' exclaimed Hopeful. 'You're in the right again, Christian, and thanks for the reminder.'

'Let's keep talking to help pass the time and stay awake,' suggested Christian. He asked his friend how he had first become a pilgrim, so Hopeful told his story.

His life in Vanity Fair had been miserable, even though he had pretended to have a good time. So he had tried very hard to be good, hoping that this would make him happy. But he hadn't succeeded. Then he'd met Faithful, who'd given him a book and told him to read it and pray.

For months he had done that, but nothing had changed. Then one day Jesus himself had come and spoken to him. Hopeful hadn't seen Jesus, but he was certain that he had come to him and said, 'Turn away from yourself and your past, and trust and obey me.'

So Hopeful had done that, and everything had changed. From that moment he had become happy, filled with love for Jesus whom he wanted to know and serve better each day for the rest of his life.

As they talked to one another of their experiences and especially of their Prince, Christian and Hopeful travelled along quite easily. Occasionally, they met and talked with other pilgrims.

And so they crossed over the Enchanted Ground and found themselves on the borders of a most attractive land.

Flatterer

Flatterer seemed friendly and helpful, but his aim was to lead pilgrims astray and trip them up. Christian and Hopeful were at a junction, wondering which path to take, when he appeared – as though sent along specially to help them! When the Flatterer offered to escort them, the pilgrims accepted eagerly.

The character of Flatterer and the little incident which follows is based on Proverbs chapter 29 verse 5.

If you read the verse in the Bible and the story you will quickly see the link.

Think about it:

Have you ever been warned about something and ignored the warning? What happened? If somebody doesn't pay attention to a warning sign who is to blame when something bad happens?

Bible Search:

Christian and Hopeful forgot some of the warnings they received. Many people tried to deceive them on the journey. But the Bible tells us that we must believe in God. Look up the following verses:

Romans 10:9   Hebrews 11:6

1 John 3:23   1 John 4:1

The City

This country was called Beulah — a wonderful place, as Christian and Hopeful found out during their stay there. The air was sweet and fresh, the sun shone day and night, the birds sang all the time and new flowers sprang up every day.

It was not at all unusual to see angels walking about the streets of Beulah, for it was on the borders of heaven. In fact, those who looked, could actually see the heavenly city. Its walls of pearls and other precious stones, and its streets of gold with the sun shining on them, were far too dazzling to look directly at, so the angels gave Christian and Hopeful special shields to cover their eyes; otherwise they might well have been blinded by the brilliance of the place. But even with these on, the sight of the city was almost too much for them at first. It made them so homesick for heaven, that they felt dizzy and faint, so that it was some time before they were able to start enjoying the beauties of Beulah.

The ground was rich and fertile, and vines, flowers and trees of all kinds grew plentifully. When they felt better, Christian and Hopeful walked to one of the vineyards and met a gardener outside it.

'Can you tell us who owns all this?' they asked him and he answered, 'The King does. He planted the trees, gardens and vineyards for his own pleasure and for the benefit of pilgrims. Come in and find out for yourselves what he provides for you.'

Then he led the way into the vineyard and invited the pilgrims to eat as many grapes as they liked. So they helped themselves and found the fruit more delicious than any they had ever tasted.

Afterwards, the man showed them round the gardens and it was in a shady spot in one of these that the pilgrims sat down to rest and soon fell asleep. But, as a side-effect of the unusual grapes they had eaten, this proved to be the most extraordinary kind of sleep, in which they were able to continue talking to one another – even more freely than they'd been doing before!

When they woke up refreshed from this wakeful-sleep, they had only one aim, and that was to reach the city – the place which had filled their thoughts and dreams all through their long and often dangerous journey. So they got up and started walking towards it.

On the way, two angels stopped them to ask where they were from and what had happened on their journey so far. The pilgrims told them and one angel answered, 'You have only two obstacles left between you and the city. Come!' Then he and his companion led Christian and Hopeful along for a while. When they stopped, the pilgrims could see very clearly the obstacles in their path. One was the heavenly gate, which was firmly shut, and the other, between them and the city, was a wide, deep, fast-flowing river. There was not a bridge or boat in sight and Christian and Hopeful were just wondering how they were going to get across, when one of the angels said, 'You have to go *through* the river to reach the gate.'

The pilgrims looked down at the water in dismay. Christian felt especially gloomy.

'Isn't there another way?' he asked.

'Not for you,' was the reply.

'Is the water the same depth all the way across?' Hopeful asked.

'No,' said one of the angels. 'But I can't tell you more than that – except that you'll find the water shallower or deeper according to your trust in the King.'

So there was nothing else for it: if the pilgrims wanted to reach the gate, and they certainly did, they would have to go through the water.

Down the bank they went – and stepped into the river. It was very deep. Hopeful found his footing quite quickly, but Christian didn't, and shouted out in panic, 'I'm sinking!'

'Steady on,' answered Hopeful bracingly. 'I'm touching the bottom and it's solid rock.'

But this was no comfort to Christian who was now in the grip of black despair and couldn't feel, hear, or see anything properly – let alone think straight.

'I'll never see the wonderful country, after all,' he wailed in despairing tones. Hopeful did his best to keep his friend's head above water and to cheer him up, but it was no use. All the wrong things he had ever done came crowding into Christian's mind. He was convinced that he was doomed, about to drown, and surrounded by evil beings all leering at him.

'Look over there, dear brother,' said Hopeful, pointing in the direction of the gate. 'I can see men waiting to welcome us.'

'To welcome *you*, you mean!' answered Christian. 'You have always been hopeful.'

'So have you – up to now!' was Hopeful's reply.

'But if I *were* fit for the city,' said Christian, 'surely my Prince would come and help me. The fact that he hasn't, proves that I'm unfit for heaven, and that I'm going to be left here to drown as a punishment for my sins!'

'You're forgetting something,' exclaimed Hopeful. 'Those who *aren't* pilgrims never have feelings like yours! No, it's only pilgrims who do! Far from deserting you, God is testing you, to see whether you'll remember how good he has been to you in the past and turn to him in your trouble now!'

A little of Hopeful's spirit began to rub off on to Christian but he still seemed dazed and shaken, until the younger man suddenly exclaimed, 'Cheer up, brother! Jesus Christ is making you whole and strong again!'

At these words a change came over Christian and everything became clear again.

'You're right!' he answered confidently. 'I can feel him close beside me again, and hear him telling me that when I go through the river, he will be with me, so I won't drown.'

As Christian said this, his feet touched the firm, solid river bed, so he began to walk boldly through the water beside Hopeful, who was very relieved that all was now well with his friend.

With each step, the water grew shallower until at last the pilgrims were standing on dry ground. Their outer clothes fell from their shoulders, and the two angels who had brought them to the river stepped forward and said, 'We have been sent to help pilgrims whom the Prince has saved. Come, we will take you to the gate.'

The city was now directly above them, at the top of a steep hill, but the climb was a pleasant one, because the angels half-carried the pilgrims up the slope. Higher and higher they climbed, through the clouds and higher still, while talking about the city just ahead.

'You'll live there for ever and be completely happy among the angels and other pilgrims,' one of the angels said. 'Best of all, you'll see the King and Prince face-to-face.'

'What will we do there?' asked Christian. The other angel answered, 'You'll serve, worship and praise the King and Prince, and this will make you happier than you could possibly imagine. And when it's time for the Prince to judge his enemies, you'll go back to earth with him and help him. Afterwards, you'll return to the city and live with everyone else in heaven in perfect love, joy and peace.'

By this time, they were close to the city, and a welcome party came out to meet them. Some of the King's trumpeters were with the group and they made music in honour of the pilgrims. Christian and Hopeful were ready to burst with happiness when they reached the heavenly gate. Here they had to stop.

Three men with very wise faces were looking down over the top of the gate. These were three famous servants of the King – Enoch, Moses and Elijah. One of the angels said to them, 'These pilgrims have come all the way from the City of Destruction because of their love for the Prince and King.' One of the men stretched out his hands and into them Christian and Hopeful placed their precious scrolls.

The great, wise men disappeared from sight, taking the scrolls with them – for they had to be presented to the King. The pilgrims waited with beating hearts. After a moment, a deep, wonderful voice could be heard saying, 'Open the gates!'

Slowly the great, shining doors opened and the pilgrims saw inside the heavenly city for the first time.

One glance, and they were changed men. Their faces shone, their eyes sparkled, and they stepped eagerly forward, past the gate and into the golden streets.

And what a welcome they received! The city's bells pealed, and the inhabitants of heaven, who had gathered to meet them, pressed round, smiling and calling out greetings or singing and making music for the new arrivals. They also gave them golden clothes, crowns and harps.

Christian and Hopeful could stay silent no longer. The words burst from them: 'Hallelujah! Praise to our Prince and King for ever and ever!' Then the gates closed behind them, and they knew they were safely home at last.

The Lord Jesus

Jesus Christ appears several times in *The Pilgrim's Progress*. Various characters throughout the book represent him. First of all there is Help who assists Christian in the Slough of Despond. Jesus Christ is our help in times of trouble and sadness. The girls in the House Beautiful mention The Lord of the Hill. Several times Jesus is refered to as a Prince, for example, the Prince of the Heavenly City.

Look up Isaiah Chapter 9 verse 6 where the prophet gives a message from God. This verse describes Jesus Christ as being a special Prince - what kind of Prince is this?

Think about it:

What do you feel like when you are going on a long journey? Are you always asking how long it is going to take? Do you breathe a sigh of relief when you arrive? If you trust in Jesus Christ you are on a journey to heaven. If you love God you will be longing to get there.

Bible Search:

All those who trust in the Lord Jesus Christ as their Saviour will be brought home to heaven when they die. Here are some verses that tell us about heaven:

Psalm 20:6

Matthew 4:17

Matthew 7:21

Matthew 18:3

Psalm 33:13

Matthew 6:19-20

Matthew 10:32

Matthew 23:9

Find out the Facts

Who was John Bunyan?

John Bunyan was a famous preacher and writer who lived in England during the fifteenth century. His most famous book is *The Pilgrim's Progress*.

John's father worked as a tinker which meant that he worked with metal. John learned to be a tinker too and worked at that until he joined Oliver Cromwell's army during the Civil War.

The King, Charles the First and Oliver Cromwell were in charge of two different armies. Charles and his army wanted kings and queens to rule the land. Oliver's army wanted the ordinary people to make the decisions. In the end Oliver Cromwell's army won and King Charles the First was captured.

What was John like when he was young?

John wasn't always a Christian. At first he did not want to obey God - he wanted to enjoy himself. Instead of learning about God he played games on the village green. He was not an educated young man and had very little learning. His family could not afford to send him to school. He did know how to read and write but didn't want to read the Bible.

Some years later however things changed for John. He realised that he was a sinner. He knew that his sin had seperated him from God and that if he was not forgiven he would not receive eternal life. He listened one day to some women talking about Jesus Christ. John could tell that these women loved Jesus and trusted in him. John began to realise that it was only through trusting in Jesus that he could be forgiven. None of John's good works would ever be good enough to get him to heaven.

What made John Bunyan write?

When he became a Christian he began to tell other people about how they needed to trust in Jesus Christ in order to be saved from their sins. John Bunyan told lots of people the good news about how they could be saved. However, this made him unpopular with the rulers of the land.

After Oliver Cromwell died Charles the First's son, Charles the Second, returned to England. He was crowned king and laws were made which said that only the king's supporters were allowed to preach. John Bunyan didn't listen to those laws and preached anyway so he was put in prison for twelve years.

While he was in prison he wrote a story about how to get to heaven. It was an adventure story as well as something that would teach people about sin, God and the Bible. It would be known as *The Pilgrim's Progress.*

John's Problems

Some people didn't think that *The Pilgrim's Progress* was John's book. They accused him of stealing it from someone else. John had to defend himself. John also wanted to be free to worship God in the way that he thought was right. But the King and other powerful people disagreed. That was why he was put in prison.

John had to provide for his family. He had a wife and children - one of whom was blind. Providing for a family was difficult for a tinker in the 1600s but it was even more difficult in prison. To make ends meet John had to make shoelaces in prison. With the little bit of money he made from making laces he was able to send some money home to feed his children.

The laws that meant that John Bunyan had to go to prison were finally changed. He was free to go home. John continued to preach but was still put back into prison for another six months. Some of his important friends however managed to get him released.

One month after John Bunyan's death a new King and Queen began to rule the United Kingdom. They supported Christians and preachers like John Bunyan. Their names were William and Mary.

New Words and Ideas

Pilgrim: This word is a name given to someone who is a traveller. They are usually religious and want to worship God. In John Bunyan's story Christian is a pilgrim travelling to the Celestial City. Christians today are referred to as pilgrims because their life is like a journey. Their destination is heaven and eternal life.

Worldly: Worldly means to love things more than you love God. If you are worldly you prefer to spend time enjoying yourself rather than enjoying the company of Jesus through praying to him and reading God's Word.

Legal: This word is used to describe something that is lawful. Legality thought you had to keep all God's laws in order to get to heaven. But no sinner can do that. The only one who kept all the law is Jesus. He is the only one who can get us to heaven. When we trust in him and in his death for us on the cross all our sin is forgiven.

Allegory: An allegory is a story with a hidden spiritual meaning. *The Pilgrim's Progress* is an allegory. Christian's burden represents the burden of sin in our lives. The book represents the Bible or God's Word which makes us aware of our sin.